© 1995 Twin Books Ltd

Produced by
TWIN BOOKS
Kimbolton House
117a Fulham Road
London SW3 6RL

Directed by CND – Muriel Nathan-Deiller
Illustrated by Van Gool-Lefèvre-Loiseaux

ISBN: 1 85469 064 7

Printed in China

Snow White
and the Seven Dwarfs

Van Gool

TWIN BOOKS

Once upon a time, in a faraway kingdom, there lived seven dwarves who had a wonderful story to tell. People came from near and far to hear how they had once rescued a beautiful Princess. And when they had finished their daily work of mining gold and precious stones, the dwarves would bring out their storybook and recall just how it had happened.

Their story began on a snowy winter's evening many years earlier, as the Queen of their land sat at her window, sewing with finely colored threads.

As she sewed, the gentle Queen pricked her finger, and a drop of her blood fell on the snow-covered windowsill. The Queen had long been hoping for a child, and she made a wish. "I wish I had a child with hair as black as night, lips as red as blood, and skin as white as snow," she said.

Later that year, a lovely daughter was born to the Queen, and all her wishes were fulfilled. The child had night-black hair, red lips, and fair skin. The happy Queen named her child Snow-white. But, sadly, the Queen died soon after her daughter was born.

After a time, the King married again.
The new Queen, too, was very beautiful, but
she was proud and cold-hearted, unlike the
mother of Snow-white.

Every day, she stood before her magic mirror and asked it the same question:
"Mirror, mirror, on the wall,
Who is the fairest of us all?"
And each day, the mirror would answer:
"Of all the beauties that were, that are,
You, O Queen, are fairest by far!"
The years went by and Snow-white grew up, becoming more beautiful with every day that passed. Her stepmother began to hate Snow-white, not only because she was beautiful, but because she was kind and good and loved by all. For years, she hid her hatred from Snow-white and her father, the King.

But one day the Queen stood before her mirror and heard a new answer to the question:

"Mirror, mirror, on the wall,
Who is the fairest of us all?"

This time the mirror replied:

"You are fair, O Queen,
 t'is true,
But Snow-white is fairer
 far than you."

The jealous Queen was enraged, and began to plot against her stepdaughter. Calling one of her huntsmen, she ordered him: "Take Snow-white deep into the forest and kill her."

The huntsman dared not disobey the Queen. Much against his will, he told Snow-white that he must go with her next time she visited the forest.

Snow-white often walked in the forest, where she could escape from the unkindness of her stepmother and the constant noise and activity of the castle. She enjoyed her quiet hours alone, but she was too kind-hearted to get the huntsman into trouble. Next time she walked in the forest, she allowed him to go with her, as her stepmother had ordered.

In a clearing far from the castle, the huntsman suddenly drew his dagger. But Snow-white was so young and beautiful that he could not carry out the Queen's order.

Confessing what had happened, the huntsman cried, "Run away! I will tell the Queen that a wild animal killed you!"
Horrified, Snow-white fled deep into the forest. Stumbling over roots and scratched by brambles, she ran until she could go no farther.

Far below, Snow-white saw a small thatched cottage nestled in a shady hollow. "Perhaps I can take shelter there," she thought. "And get something to eat before I go on." From a distance, the small animals of the forest watched and wondered.

Snow-white walked down the hill and
knocked timidly at the door of the cottage.
When there was no answer, she let herself in.

To Snow-white's surprise, everything in the cottage was very small—the cups, the knives and forks, even the beds. She poured herself a cup of milk and ate a slice of bread.

Then she lay down on one of the little beds and fell asleep at once.

Late that afternoon the seven dwarves shouldered their tools and left the mine.

In an orderly line, according to the numbers on their hats, they filed through the forest until they reached their cottage.

"Here's to a hearty meal and a good night's rest," cried Dwarf Number One. But he stopped in surprise when he saw that the cottage door was wide open.

Alarmed, the dwarves peeked inside their cottage. But instead of a burglar, they saw a beautiful young girl sound asleep on one of their beds, just as if she belonged there!

"Who can this be?" the dwarves asked one another. But the only way to find out was to awaken their unexpected visitor. When Snow-white told the little men about her stepmother's wicked plot, they were shocked. Her gentleness and beauty won them over at once.

25

"You may stay with us as long as you like," the dwarves promised Snow-white. "Your wicked stepmother will never find you here." Snow-white was very happy to meet with such kindness after the cruel treatment she had received from her stepmother. "I will cook and clean and mend for you," she promised the dwarves. "Thank you for letting me stay." Then she set the table for dinner and they celebrated their new friendship with a party.

The next morning, Snow-white made a delicious breakfast of pancakes, fresh eggs, ham, and buttered toast. The dwarves set off for their mine well fed and in high spirits. "Now be careful of strangers," they called back to Snow-white. "Don't speak to anyone whom you don't know."

"I won't," she answered, waving goodbye.

At the castle, the wicked Queen was standing before her magic mirror.

Sure that Snow-white was dead, her jealous stepmother asked again, "Who is the fairest of us all?" She was enraged when the mirror replied:

"Queen, thou art of beauty rare,
But Snow-white, living in the glen,
With the seven little men,
Is a thousand times more fair."
Disguising herself as an old peasant in a
mask and ragged clothes, the Queen brewed a
deadly poison. Into it, she dipped a basketful
of bright red apples.

By means of magic the Queen learned the way to the dwarves' cottage. There, late in the day, she found Snow-white.

"Good day, my child," she said in a feeble, trembling voice. "Would you like a ripe apple?"

The apple looked so good that Snow-white forgot the dwarves' warning against strangers. And her kindness made her unwilling to refuse the poor old woman's gift.

"Thank you," she replied. And she took a bite of the poisoned fruit.

Immediately, Snow-white fell to the ground as if she were dead.

The wicked Queen laughed with pleasure. "Now I need not trust my servants to obey me," she said. "I have gotten rid of you myself, and I am surely the fairest in the land."

Just as the Queen turned back toward the castle, the seven dwarves came home and saw Snow-white lying beside the spilled basket of fruit.

"Who are you?" they demanded of the old woman. "And what have you done to our Princess?"

The Queen turned and fled, pursued by the angry dwarves. They were determined to avenge Snow-white, who remained motionless on the ground.

The dwarves were small in body but fierce in anger. They ran after the Queen until she had to stop for breath above a swift stream. There they threw their war clubs at her and pushed her into the torrent. Her magic was no help to her. The jealous Queen was swept away, never to be seen again in that land.

The dwarves hurried home, but hope died in them when they found Snow-white lying where she had fallen. They gathered around her still form and wept. It was hard to believe that her youth and beauty had been destroyed in a moment by her jealous stepmother.

Using their great skill as metalworkers, the dwarves fashioned a gleaming casket of gold and crystal. Sadly, they placed Snow-white in the casket and set it atop a high hill. For many days and nights, they kept a vigil beside it.

One day, the handsome Prince of a nearby kingdom noticed the beautiful crystal-and-gold casket shining in the sun. He rode closer and saw that it contained a beautiful young woman.

The dwarves told him the sad story, and the Prince, too, began to weep. "She is so beautiful," he said. "Let me just kiss her once before I go."

The dwarves agreed and opened the casket so that the Prince could gather Snow-white in his arms. But as soon as he did so, her eyelids fluttered and she awoke from her long trance. "Where am I?" she asked.

Overjoyed, the Prince and the dwarves told Snow-white all that had happened since she had taken a bite of the poisoned apple.

"Come with me to my father's castle," said the Prince, "and you shall be my bride."

The dwarves were delighted that Snow-white had awakened to a new life. They danced at the wedding of their Princess and her Prince. And the happy couple never forgot the seven friends who had destroyed the wicked Queen and brought them together.